For Sara, Jean, and May

Hello Baby

By Charlotte Doyle
Illustrated by Kees de Kiefte

Random House New York

Text copyright © 1989 by Charlotte Doyle. Illustrations copyright © 1989 by Kees de Kiefte. All rights reserved under International and Pan-American Copyright Conventions. Published in the United States by Random House, Inc., New York, and simultaneously in Canada by Random House of Canada Limited, Toronto.

Library of Congress Cataloging-in-Publication Data:
Doyle, Charlotte. Hello baby / by Charlotte Doyle ; illustrated by Kees de Kiefte. p. cm.—(A Just right book) SUMMARY: Homer discovers what babies can and cannot do when his mother brings home his new brother Leo. ISBN: 0-394-80265-9 (trade); 0-394-90265-3 (lib. bdg.) [1. Babies—Fiction. 2. Brothers—Fiction] I. Kiefte, Kees de, ill. II. Title. III. Series: Just right book (New York, N.Y.) PZ7.C38135He 1989 [E]—dc19 88-6731

Manufactured in the United States of America 1 2 3 4 5 6 7 8 9 0

JUST RIGHT BOOKS is a trademark of Random House, Inc.

One day Homer's mom came home with a new baby.
The baby's name was Leo. Baby Leo was one week old.
   Homer asked his mom, "Why are you carrying that baby?"
   Homer's mom said, "You know what? Babies can't walk."

Homer wanted to say hello.

He went up to the baby and said: "Hello baby."

The baby did not say anything.

Homer said, "Hello baby. Hello baby."

The baby did not say anything.

Homer's dad said, "Babies can't talk."

Baby Leo began to cry.
Homer's dad said, "I think Baby Leo is hungry."
Homer ran and got Baby Leo an apple.
Homer's dad said, "Babies can't bite or chew. They don't have any teeth."

Homer watched his mom feed Baby Leo.

After a while Homer smelled something. Homer's mom smelled it too.

Homer's mom said, "Well, well, well, and what do you know? I think Baby Leo made a mess in his pants."

Homer said, "You know what? Yuck."

Homer's dad took Baby Leo out to change his diaper.

Homer climbed on his mom's lap.

He said to his mom, "You know what? Babies can't do much."

Homer's mom said, "That's true. But do you know what? I was once a baby, and so were you."

Homer pretended to cry like a baby. Homer's mom rocked him. She pretended to feed him from a pretend bottle.

Homer grew tired of playing baby. He jumped off his mom's lap and began to sing and dance. He danced all the way to his room. Homer picked up Booboo the Blue-Eyed Bear and danced around with him and sang:

"Babies can't talk and babies can't walk.
Babies can't dance. They mess in their pants.
Babies can't chew and babies can't sing.
Babies can hardly do anything.
No, there's not much a baby can do.
But I was once a baby, and so were you."

Days went by: Sunday, Monday, Tuesday, Wednesday, Thursday, Friday, Saturday. Baby Leo was two weeks old. Homer wanted to say hello. Homer said, "Hello baby."

Baby Leo's eyes were shut.
Homer said, "Hello baby. Hello baby."
The baby didn't say anything.
Homer tickled Baby Leo.
Baby Leo cried.
Homer was upset.

Homer's mom was upset too. She said, "Well, well, well. What's going on here? What did you do to the baby?"

Homer said, "I tickled him."

Homer's mom said, "You know what? You have to be very careful with the baby. When you are all alone with him, better keep your hands to yourself."

Homer went to his room.
He tickled Booboo the Blue-Eyed Bear.
Then he dunked Booboo in the trash can.

Homer fished Booboo out of the trash can and shook the dirt off him. As he shook Booboo, Homer said:

"Babies can't talk and babies can't walk.
Babies can't dance. They mess in their pants.
Babies can't chew and babies can't sing.
Babies can hardly do anything.
No, there's not much a baby can do.
But I was once a baby, and so were you."

Days went by: Sunday, Monday, Tuesday, Wednesday, Thursday, Friday, Saturday. Baby Leo was three weeks old. Homer's dad was asleep on the couch.

Homer did not want to wake up his dad.

Very quietly, Homer tiptoed over to visit Baby Leo.
Baby Leo looked and looked at Homer.
Homer looked and looked at Baby Leo. Homer wanted to tickle Baby Leo, but Homer kept his hands to himself.

Homer wanted to say hello, but he did not want to wake up his dad. Hardly making a sound, Homer opened his mouth wide and shut it as if to whisper, "Hello baby. Hello baby. Hello baby."

Baby Leo looked and looked at Homer's mouth.

Homer opened his mouth again and again as if to say, "Hello baby. Hello baby. Hello baby."

Baby Leo looked and looked. Then Baby Leo's arms began to shake. Baby Leo's head shook. Baby Leo was trying to do something.

Baby Leo's mouth opened and shut and opened and shut as if to say, "Ahm. Ahm."

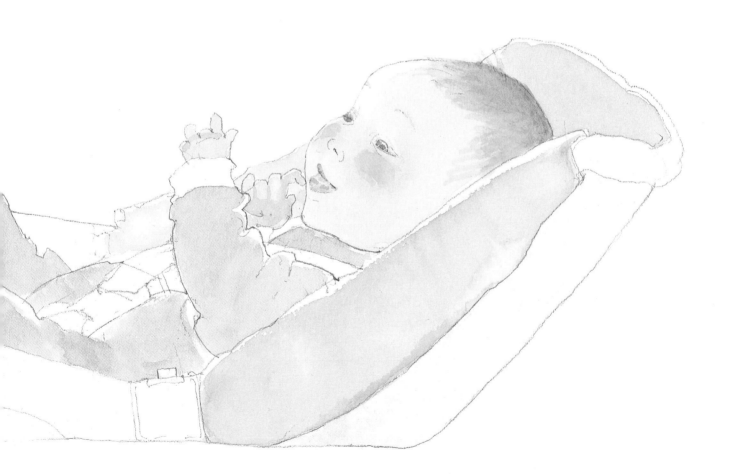

Homer smiled. Baby Leo was trying to say hello!

Homer whispered, "Hello baby," and tiptoed to his room.

Homer whispered, "Hello baby" to Booboo the Blue-Eyed Bear. He rocked Booboo on his knee and whispered:

"Well, well, well, and what do you know?
Today my baby brother tried to say hello.
But babies can't talk and babies can't walk.
Babies can't dance. They mess in their pants.
Babies can't chew and babies can't sing.
Babies can hardly do anything. But...
Well, well, well, and what do you know?
Today my baby brother tried to say hello."

Homer put Booboo on the bed and lay down.
"Hello baby," whispered Homer, and put his arms around
Booboo. Soon Homer was fast asleep.